Old Thomas

AND THE LITTLE FAIRY

Canadian Cataloguing in Publication Data
Demers, Dominique
(Vieux Thomas et la petite fée. English)
Old Thomas and the Little Fairy
Translation of: Vieux Thomas et la petite fée.

ENGLISH TEXT: SHEILA FISCHMAN

ISBN 1-894363-45-0

I. Fischman, Sheila II. Poulin, Stéphane
III. Title. IV. Title: Vieux Thomas et la petite fée.
English.

PS8557.E4683V5313 2000 jC813'.54 C00-900498-X
PZ7.D3921201 2000

Publisher: Dominique Payette
Series Editor: Lucie Papineau
Graphic Design: Primeau & Barey

Legal Deposit: 3rd Quarter 2000
Bibliothèque nationale du Québec
National Library of Canada

Dominique & Friends
Canada:
300 Arran Street, Saint Lambert,
Quebec, Canada, J4R 1K5

USA:
P.O. Box 800
Champlain, New York
12919

Tel: 1-888-228-1498
Fax: 1-888-782-1481
E-mail:
dominique.friends@editionsheritage.com

Printed in China
10 9 8 7 6 5 4 3

The publisher wishes to thank the Canada
Council for its support, as well as SODEC and
Canadian Heritage.

*To Lucie Papineau
in friendship
D.D.*

*To Marilou
S.P.*

Old Thomas

AND THE LITTLE FAIRY

Text: Dominique Demers
Illustrations: Stéphane Poulin

Old Thomas may not have seen his hundredth birthday yet but he was
very, very old. He lived alone among the gulls and the cormorants.
He no longer fished. Old Thomas was angry at the whole world.
One evening when he was pacing the beach and shouting insults at the
stars and the waves, he discovered a tiny little girl who had been
washed up on the sand.

She was hardly any bigger than a matchstick. Her skin was cold and her clothes in tatters, but her heart was still beating. Old Thomas scooped her up in his big hand. She just lay still and he had the impression that she didn't weigh a thing.

Old Thomas had vowed that never again would he mix with human beings. They had caused him too much pain. But then, the little girl in the palm of his hand was exceptionally small. "If I just leave her there," he thought, "the sea will swallow her up at the first tide."

As fierce winds battered his cabin, Old Thomas
set about to save the little girl. He laid her down
in a pearly shell and tore strips of cloth from
his shirt to make covers for her. Then, slowly and
patiently, he dribbled drops of rain water
between her lips.

For three nights and as many days he watched over her. The little girl's heart was still fluttering but her eyes remained closed and all her limbs were motionless. The old man was desperate.

When the sun reappeared, Old Thomas went outside to shout insults at it. But the old fisherman discovered that his rage had left him. He was a different man now. He closed his eyes, breathed in the salty air and murmured a secret prayer to the sun, the sea and the wind.

When he came back, the little girl had opened her eyes.

The old man started fishing again. He brought his tiny
protégée fishes that were long and shiny and had the most
delicious flesh. And just for her, he explored the shore
in search of small sweet fruit.

"I'm going to be enormous!" protested the little girl,
laughing. With relish, she swallowed tiny mouthfuls.

When he looked at her, Old Thomas could feel his
heart dancing. Sometimes he even caught himself thinking:
"I wonder if she might be a fairy?"

That evening, instead of brooding over dark thoughts, Old Thomas listened to the song of the waves and gazed at his little fairy as she skipped under the stars. He was happy.

One morning when Thomas was at sea, a stray dog that was starving picked up the child's scent.

Old Thomas had just caught a magnificent fish with fins of silver and gold when a terrible foreboding swept over him. He abandoned his catch and rowed with all his might towards the shore.

The little girl had heard the wild dog growling.
Bravely she climbed up to the one shelf in the cabin
and hid herself. She was trembling all over as
she imagined the breath of the dog, his rough tongue,
and his pointed teeth as shiny as a quarter moon.

The closer Old Thomas came, the more he felt panic rising in him. His little fairy was in danger. He was sure of it.

With a powerful lunge, the dog pushed open the door. Just inside he found a basin filled with fine fat fish, but they didn't interest him in the least. The wicked beast was haunted by the exquisite fragrance of the tiny girl.

The animal prowled about with his tail down, ears up, muzzle quivering. He began to claw the ground beneath the shelf, and he let out a terrible, piercing howl like the cry of a wolf.

Then suddenly he leaped up and knocked down the shelf.

Old Thomas spied the wild dog first. And then his little fairy lying on the ground among the shattered dishes. Listening only to his courage, he threw himself at the animal, which was foaming with rage.

The little girl had fainted away in fright. When she came to,
the beast had fled. Old Thomas was lying on the ground, his body
cruelly marked by the horrible dog's claws and fangs. The tiny child
climbed onto the old man's chest and pressed her ear against it.
Old Thomas's heart was still beating faintly.

Making extraordinary efforts, the little girl
cleaned Old Thomas's wounds and gave
him something to drink. She even brought
him fish and small sweet fruit. But he
wanted none of it.

He knew that he was going to die.
And he felt ready. He no longer wanted
to insult the moon or the sea, the sun or
the wind. His little fairy was there at
his side, safe and sound and wonderfully
alive. Old Thomas was content.

At nightfall, he got up laboriously and slowly walked towards the sea. It was there that he wanted to disappear, among the fishes with luminous scales and the buried shells.

Soon a tall wave carried him away. At the same moment hundreds of sea birds – gulls, plovers, cormorants – gave a heartrending cry.

Little by little, the sea withdrew, leaving behind on the shore multicoloured pebbles, ribbons of seaweed and pearly nuggets.

Aside from that, the beach was deserted.
The little girl had disappeared.